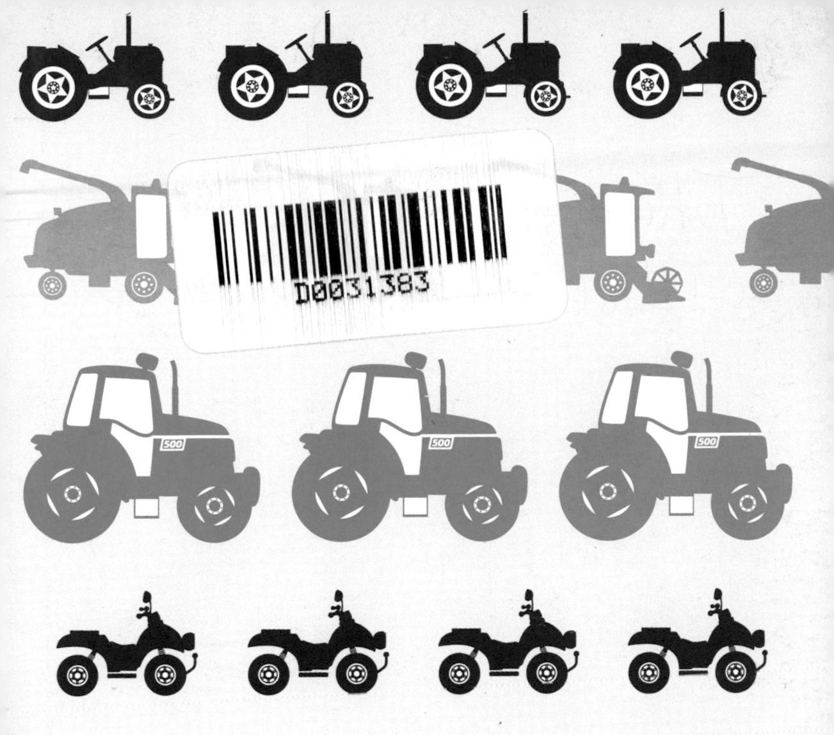
500
500
500

500
500
500

This book belongs to: Arantx Carrillo

A catalogue record for this book is available from the British Library

Adapted from the television script by Keith Littler, based on the original stories by Colin Reader.

Photographs by James Lampard.

Published by Ladybird Books Ltd.
80 Strand, London, WC2R 0RL
A Penguin Company

4 6 8 10 9 7 5

ISBN-13: 978-1-84422-696-2
ISBN-10: 1-8442-2696-4

Printed in China

The Beast Of Babblebrook

It was a glorious summer's day at Gosling Farm. Stan decided it was the perfect weather to give Patch a bath. Little Red Tractor watched as the tub filled up with bubbles.

"I know you don't like it, but you're starting to smell," Stan explained to his sheepdog.

Stan went into the barn to turn off the tap. By the time he got back, Patch was gone!

"Don't tell me he's run off," groaned Stan.

"Toot! Toot!" parped Little Red Tractor.

LRT1

"Rooaaar!"

Ryan and Amy raced into the yard. They were very excited because they were planning a camping trip.

"Save me!" Amy giggled, hiding behind Little Red Tractor's shiny front wheel.

"What are you two up to?" asked Stan.

"I'm pretending to be the Beast of Babblebrook," said Ryan.

"We always tell scary stories when we go camping," added Amy.

"Can we camp on your land?" asked Ryan.

Stan nodded. "I'm having an evening in, so Little Red Tractor and I will be here if you need us."

Mr Jones and Big Blue were out in the fields of Beech Farm.

"This new muck spreader works a treat," chuckled Mr Jones.

"Honk!" agreed Big Blue, as smelly manure splattered behind them.

As they crossed the lane to the next field, Mr Jones decided to save some time. "We'll leave the spreader on."

He looked left and right. "No one's about. Come on."

But someone WAS about... Stumpy!

"Morning Mr Jo..." smiled Stumpy, not noticing the clods of muck flying through the air.

"Woah!" he cried, as Nipper zigzagged out of control, straight into a stone wall! Poor Stumpy was sent flying.

As Nipper rolled down the lane, Stumpy picked himself up. He was covered from head to foot in stinky muck.

"I can't see a thing, it's all in my eyes," he cried. He stumbled forward, straight into a patch of nettles. "Ouch!"

Walter and Rusty came spluttering up the lane.

BANG! Suddenly the old car ground to a halt.

"Why, why, why? When we're so close to home..." wailed Walter.

Then he saw a strange figure staggering towards them.

"It's the Beast of Babblebrook," cried Walter. "We've got to get out of here!"

But Rusty refused to start.

To Walter's alarm, the figure started to get closer! Then Rusty decided it was time to go. Vroom!

Stumpy heard the racket as the pair sped off. "Hello? Are you there Walter?"

By the time he got back to the garage, Walter was in a terrible state.

"The Beast! I've seen the Beast of Babblebrook."

"You can't have, that's just an old story," said Stan. He'd come to rent a DVD to watch that evening.

But Walter wasn't taking any chances.
"I'm locking myself and Nicola inside the garage."
Stan climbed aboard Little Red Tractor, then waved goodbye to Nicola.
"Perhaps your dad did see something," he said. "We'll check our cows just in case."

Back at Beech Farm, Mr Jones and Big Blue had nearly finished.

"One more load should cover it," Mr Jones decided.

Before the pair could fetch any more muck, the farmer spotted something odd through his binoculars.

A shadowy shape was moving across the field – straight towards them!

Mr Jones was terrified. "It's the Beast of Babblebrook."

There was only one thing to do.

"We must hide until it goes away! Come on Big Blue."

When Stan and Little Red Tractor arrived at the field, there wasn't a beast in sight.

"Let's get home and see if we can finish bathing Patch," said Stan.

Further up the road, Little Red Tractor tooted hello to Nipper.

"Why would Stumpy leave Nipper out here?" Stan wondered. "I'd better move him out of the road."

Ryan and Amy arrived just as Little Red Tractor was towing Nipper along.

"Mum won't let us go camping now," sighed Amy. Walter had told Laura Turvey about the Beast of Babblebrook.

"Ask Mr Jones to go with you," said Stan. "I'm sure your mum would be fine with that."

Back at Beech Garage, Mr Jones and Walter swapped scary stories. They then both decided to hide until the Beast was caught. Mr Jones refused to even answer his front door to Ryan and Amy.

"Go home and don't talk to any strange monsters on the way," Mr Jones shouted through the letterbox.

"Grown ups are weird," said Ryan.

Luckily Stan saved the day.

"Camp here in the barn and Little Red Tractor can keep an eye on you."

That night, while Stan settled down to his film, Amy and Ryan told spooky stories in their tent outside.

"Then there was a scratching at the door and..."

Suddenly, they heard a CRASH!

Ryan poked his head out of the tent.

"There's something out there."

"It's the Beast!" whispered Amy, "and it's heading right for us."

The pair hid behind Little Red Tractor.

"Help us," begged Ryan.

Ryan and Amy gasped as a dark figure staggered into the farmyard.

Little Red Tractor blasted the loudest toot he could make.

"Wha...?" growled the figure.

The Beast was getting closer and closer.

Then there was a loud SPLASH!

Stan came running out of the farmhouse.
"What's going on?"
"Little Red Tractor has caught the Beast of Babblebrook," cried Ryan.
Stan switched on Little Red Tractor's headlights.
"He's definitely caught something..."

"Stumpy!?" shouted Ryan, Amy and Stan all together.

Poor Stumpy had tripped and fallen into Patch's tin bath.

"You wouldn't believe the day I've had!" Stumpy said. "I've even managed to lose Nipper."

"Don't worry, Nipper's safe and sound," said Stan.

"What is that smell?" asked Ryan.

"It must have been you that Walter saw wandering around the field," realised Stan.

Amy giggled. "Stumpy is the Beast of Babblebrook!"

"And Little Red Tractor saved us all," added Ryan.

"You're our hero Little Red Tractor!" said Amy, giving him a big hug.

"Toot! Toot!" beeped Little Red Tractor happily.

500
500
500

500
500
500